Then he held her close whom he loved the most.
He threw her up and caught her.

'She's the sweetest girl in all the world.

She's my darling daughter!'

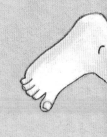

he told the
cow and the cat,
the pig,
duck, and hen.

'Oh, thank you, thank you,
and thank you again,'

...what a surprise!
'You found my darling daughter!'

rubbed his eyes and ...

Poppa Bombola rubbed his eyes –

but he'd lost his darling daughter.

Poppa Bombola sat down and cried – he covered his
eyes and he cried and he cried.

'Oh, where's my
darling daughter?'

He'd searched his farm high and low.
Everywhere he'd sought her.
He knew he'd put her somewhere safe,

'Oh, where's my darling daughter?'

Poppa Bombola ran to the sty –
ran to the sty with tears in his eyes.
'I've lost my daughter,' he told the pig.

'I'm running around, all in a tizz.
Do you know where my daughter is?
I'm sure I put her somewhere safe.

'I've lost my daughter,' he told the hen,
and then he bolted off again.

'I know I put her somewhere safe.
Oh, where's my darling daughter?'

Poppa Bombola ran to the pen –
ran to the pen with his
hair all on end.

I know I put her somewhere safe.
Oh, where's my darling daughter?'

Poppa Bombola ran to the shed –
ran to the shed with his heart full of dread.
'I've lost my daughter,' he told the cow.
'Don't ask me how – I haven't
got time to talk to you now.

'I've lost my daughter,' he told the duck,
as he waded and wallowed
and slipped in the muck.

'I know I put her somewhere safe.
Oh, where's my
darling daughter?'

Poppa Bombola ran to the pond –
right into the pond with
his best boots on.

He looked under
the cat!

'I know I put her somewhere safe.
Oh, where's my darling daughter?'

Poppa Bombola ran out the back –
ran out the back in a terrible flap.
'I've lost my daughter,' he told the cat.
He looked under the mat.

He looked everywhere.
High and low he sought her.
'I know I put her somewhere safe,
but I've lost my darling daughter!'

He looked on the table and under the chairs.

Poppa Bombola
looked in the cot –
looked in the cot and
got such a shock!

'Where's my darling
daughter?'

# Quack Quack Moo, We See You!

Written by
Mij Kelly

Illustrated by
Katharine McEwen

OXFORD
UNIVERSITY PRESS

To Briony – M.K.

For Emilia, with lots of love – K.M.

## OXFORD
### UNIVERSITY PRESS

Great Clarendon Street, Oxford OX2 6DP

Oxford University Press is a department of the University of Oxford.
It furthers the University's objective of excellence in research, scholarship,
and education by publishing worldwide in

Oxford   New York

Auckland   Cape Town   Dar es Salaam   Hong Kong   Karachi
Kuala Lumpur   Madrid   Melbourne   Mexico City   Nairobi
New Delhi   Shanghai   Taipei   Toronto

With offices in

Argentina   Austria   Brazil   Chile   Czech Republic   France   Greece
Guatemala   Hungary   Italy   Japan   Poland   Portugal   Singapore
South Korea   Switzerland   Thailand   Turkey   Ukraine   Vietnam

Oxford is a registered trade mark of Oxford University Press
in the UK and in certain other countries

British Library Cataloguing in Publication Data
Data available
ISBN: 978-0-19-275746-3 (paperback)

1 3 5 7 9 10 8 6 4 2

Printed in China

Paper used in the production of this book is a natural, recyclable product
made from wood grown in sustainable forests. The manufacturing process
conforms to the environmental regulations of the country of origin.